CONTENTS

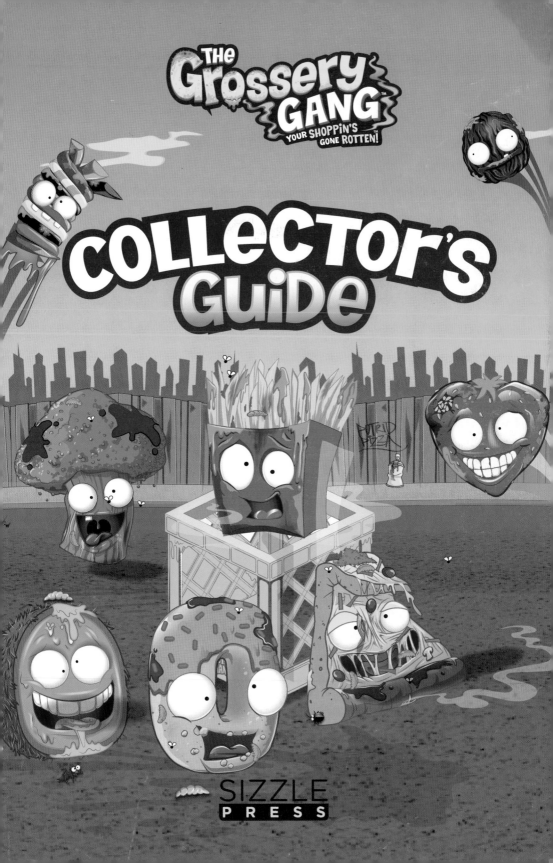

SIZZLE
PRESS

An imprint of Bonnier Publishing USA
251 Park Avenue South, New York, NY 10010

Manufactured in China HH 0617
First Edition 2 4 6 8 10 9 7 5 3 1
ISBN 978-1-4998-0657-1
sizzlepressbooks.com
bonnierpublishingusa.com

Under license by:
©2017 Moose Enterprise (INT) Pty Ltd. Grossery Gang™ logos,
names, and characters are licensed trademarks of Moose
Enterprise (INT) Pty Ltd.
29 Grange Road, Cheltenham, VIC 3192, Australia
www.moosetoys.com
info@moosetoys.com

The Grossery Gang lives in an oddball, gross, and wacky world of retail, shops, and stores where all the shopping goods are starting to rot!

This crusty crew of putrid products have hit their expiration dates and festered to life to create their own brand of filthy fun!

There are over 150 characters to find at the Yucky Mart, including Putrid Pizza, Dodgey Donut, Shoccoli, Rotten Egg, and more! The fun times (and fragrant fumes) never stop when the Grossery Gang's involved! So come on down to the Yucky Mart to hang out with the grossest of gangs—and see if you can collect them all!

The Yucky Mart

Welcome to the Yucky Mart—where stale's on sale and sold comes with mold! Browse the aisles of putrid products and foul foods! It's your one slop shop where the shoppin's gone rotten!

The Yucky Mart can be found in Cheap Town, a once-bustling neighborhood of various stores—but not since the mega motorway to Sales City was built!

Don't feel bad though, SOMETHING has been left behind…take a peek inside the Yucky Mart and you might just catch the Grossery Gang hanging out in the vile aisles!

Gross Gang

Likes: Experiments
Dislikes: Toast
May Contain Traces Of:
Manure, worms, and slugs!
Rarity: Ultra rare

SHOCCOLI

He may have a wilted head and an offensive smell, but Shoccoli still fancies himself the brains of the gang—and considering the other members, who are we to argue?

Constantly tinkering on new, insane inventions using stuff he scavenges from the store, Shoccoli (aka Doc Brocc) never fails to whip up miracles of mad science—or zap himself silly when he flicks the switch—just as all hope seems lost!

STiCKY SODa

Lighthearted, friendly, and positively upbeat are not the kinds of words anyone would use to describe Sticky Soda.

A soda whose fizz ran out long ago, Sticky Soda (aka Sparkles) walks on the dry side with a hilariously acidic aftertaste. What she lacks in sweetness, she more than makes up for in savvy sarcasm and biting retorts.

Likes: Bubbles
Dislikes: Dentists
May contain Traces of: Fish, vomit, and stale water!
Rarity: Common

PUTRID PIZZA

Putrid Pizza, the Slice with Lice, the Big Cheese—this charismatic but putrid piece of pizza pie goes by many names, but the only one that seems to stick (to the floor, mostly) is Pizza Face!

Pizza Face is the never-say-die leader of this ragtag crew, a congealed mastermind who loves nothing more than to find fun in the unlikeliest (and grossest) of places.

Likes: Practical jokes

Dislikes: Heights

May Contain Traces Of: Mold, slime, and bacteria!

Rarity: Common

Likes: Partying
Dislikes: Getting dunk'd
May contain traces of: Rocks, trash, and bugs!
Rarity: Common

Dodgey Donut

He's as hard as a rock and he loves to roll! Dodgey Donut (aka Rocky) is the wildest party animal in the aisle! Rude, crude and barely food, Dodgey Donut's priorities in life are partying, partying, and partying—not necessarily in that order.

But when the chips are down (and they often are after Rocky knocks every bag off the shelves), this bodacious baked good is the one you want on your side!

GROSS GANG

ROTTEN EGG

Fart your day with a Rotten Egg! The last to have expired and therefore the youngest of the group, Rotten Egg (aka Egghead) is in a constant struggle to catch up with his peers.

The freshman of the group, Egghead may be a bit slow, but that doesn't stop him from jumping into the gang's adventures headfirst! Or feetfirst. Especially since he forgets which is which. Hey, he's round!

Likes: Farts
Dislikes: Boiling water
May Contain Traces of: Feathers, beaks, and nasty smells!
Rarity: Common

LikeS: Ketchup

DiSLikeS: Vegetables

MaY CONTaiN TraCeS OF: Rotten potatoes, oil, and fried flies!

RariTY: Common

FuNGuS FrieS

Surprisingly nutty for a box of spuds, Fungus Fries is proof that you don't need to be crazy to live in the Yucky Mart—but it sure helps. This merry madman can often be found shouting out barely intelligible sentences.

Fungus's impulsive insanity has a tendency to ruin the gang's best-laid plans, but they can't stay mad at the loopy tuber for long—he's just so happy! All the time. So, so happy. It's unnerving, really.

Gross Greasies

Horrid Hamburger

It's not just the pickle that's green!

Likes: Pickles and mustard
Dislikes: Veggie burgers
May contain traces of: Mold, dead animal, and sneeze!
Rarity: Common

Burp-rito

He's the snack that makes you burp till it hurts!

Likes: Chihuahuas
Dislikes: Salad
May contain traces of: Gas, farts, and Chihuahua!
Rarity: Common

Stinki

He's the souvlaki full of ooze
that you don't want to choose!

Likes: Pickles
Dislikes: Olives
May Contain Traces Of:
Pus, scabs, and plastic!
Rarity: Common

Toxic Taco

His toxic taste will
take your breath away!

Likes: Worms
Dislikes: Mild salsa
May Contain Traces Of:
Cheese, dirt, and maggots!
Rarity: Common

HaLF BaKeD BaKery

BarF BaGeL

He's a hole lot of mold
that tastes really old!

Likes: Pastrami
Dislikes: Donut holes
May Contain Traces Of:
Grime, vomit, and dribble!
Rarity: Rare

YuCK ÉCLaire

He's moldy and creamy and
makes your poop dreamy!

Likes: Curdled cream
Dislikes: Iced buns
May Contain Traces Of:
Bacteria, chocolate,
and eyelashes!
Rarity: Rare

PUTRiD PANCAKES

He's the stack that'll make you yak!

Likes: Syrup and sugar
DisLikes: Blowin' his stack
May Contain Traces Of: Butter, drool, and rotten fruit!
Rarity: Common

AWFUL WAFFLE

He'll sit in your gut and make you throw up!

Likes: Getting toasted
DisLikes: Anything fresh
May Contain Traces Of: Butter, slime, and grime!
Rarity: Common

HALF Baked Bakery

Knot Nice Pretzel

He's the pretzel that's knot nice, knot tasty, and knot edible!

Likes: Karaoke
Dislikes: Slugs
May Contain Traces Of: Knots, rope, and twine!
Rarity: Common

Stale Muffin

He's the muffin top that smells like a bottom!

Likes: Chocolate chips
Dislikes: Mornings
May Contain Traces Of: Sawdust, leaves, and meat!
Rarity: Common

Pukey Cookie

He's the cookie that's chewy and just a touch spewy!

Likes: Milk
Dislikes: Santa Claus
May Contain Traces Of: Puke, flies, and dog hair!
Rarity: Common

Ginger Dread Man

You can catch him like a bad cold!

Likes: Gum drops
Dislikes: Summer
May Contain Traces Of: Sugar, mice, and slime!
Rarity: Ultra rare

Chunky Cheesecake

He's moldy and cheesy and makes you feel queasy!

Likes: Pedicures
Dislikes: Mice
May Contain Traces Of: Mouse poop, toenails, and cake!
Rarity: Rare

Badly Frozen

Unfrozen Pizza

Will you get the slice that's actually nice?

Likes: Purple pepperoni
Dislikes: Ovens
May Contain Traces Of: Warts, dust, and fingernails!
Rarity: Rare

Maggot Milk

His maggots might make you cry!

Likes: Cereal
Dislikes: Cheese
May Contain Traces Of: Grass, gunk, and weevils!
Rarity: Rare

Frozen Foul

He's the chicken that doesn't taste like chicken!

Likes: Vegetarians
Dislikes: Christmas
May Contain Traces Of:
Gizzards, claws, and feathers!
Rarity: Rare

Yuck TV Dinner

He's the tray full of muck that tastes really yuck!

Likes: Watching TV
Dislikes: Commercials
May Contain Traces Of:
Tin, mice, and batteries!
Rarity: Rare

Scummy Sodas

Flat Fizz

Flat and queasy for you
to drink easy!

Likes: Sugar

Dislikes: Stilettos

May contain traces of:
Bubbles, sugar, and more sugar!

Rarity: Rare

Sweaty Sports Drink

Need an energy boost? You'd
better choose any drink but him!

Likes: Exhaustion

Dislikes: Water

May contain traces of:
Tears, sugar, and sweat!

Rarity: Common

Yuck Yogurt

He's a tub of grubs that really grows on you!

Likes: Mold
Dislikes: Lumps
May Contain Traces of: Bacteria, beetles, and tissues!
Rarity: Common

Stinky Cheese

He tastes like mold and smells really old!

Likes: Crackers
Dislikes: Deodorant
May Contain Traces of: Mice, holes, and mold!
Rarity: Common

Cruddy Cream

He's the cream that got left behind.

Likes: Strawberries
Dislikes: Heat
May Contain Traces of: Grit, lumps, and straw!
Rarity: Ultra rare

Barf-Room Supplies

Icky Eyedrops

He's sticky and grim and he'll make your eyes sting!

Likes: Eye gunk

Dislikes: Contact lenses

May Contain Traces Of: Flies, salt, and slime!

Rarity: Common

Rough Toilet Paper

He's the roughest toilet paper around! No butts about it!

Likes: Poop

Dislikes: Getting flushed

May Contain Traces Of: Sandpaper, cardboard, and splinters!

Rarity: Rare

GROTTY SOAP

He's the soap that's green and feels very unclean!

Likes: Soap scum

Dislikes: Water

May Contain Traces Of: Fat, dirt, and sour cream!

Rarity: Rare

SPOTTY ZIT CREAM

He makes you look zitty and feel really gritty!

Likes: Popping zits

Dislikes: Facials

May Contain Traces Of: Pus, toads, and warts!

Rarity: Common

Barf-Room Supplies

SHAMPOOP

He's the 2-in-1 Shampoop that gives you tangles and tears!

Likes: Showers
Dislikes: Lice
May Contain Traces Of: Onions, poop, and shaving cream!
Rarity: Rare

ROTTING TOOTHPASTE

He's the stinky way to cause decay! Now in new garlic flavor!

Likes: Cavities
Dislikes: Dentists
May Contain Traces Of: Sugar, candy, and soda!
Rarity: Rare

SNOT GOOD TISSUES

He's snot good, snot soft, and snot nice to use!

Likes: Sneezes
Dislikes: Toilets
May Contain Traces of: Snot, boogers, and mucus!
Rarity: Rare

SPLODGY SPRAY CAN

His spray is all gloopy to make you smell poopy!

Likes: Bathrooms
Dislikes: Air freshener
May Contain Traces of: Metal, gas, and cockroaches!
Rarity: Common

Awful Sauces

Vile Vinegar

He's so vile, you can smell him for miles!

Likes: Chips
Dislikes: Cupcakes
May Contain Traces of: Mice, rice, and acid!
Rarity: Common

Disgusting Mustard

He's the moldy mustard that will make you disgusted!

Likes: Hot dogs
Dislikes: Onions
May Contain Traces of: Grease, dirt, and car fumes!
Rarity: Common

Bad Soy

He's the slimy soy that brings no joy!

Likes: Raw fish
Dislikes: Fast food
May Contain Traces Of:
Oil, grumpiness, and nose hair!
Rarity: Common

Burnt BBQ Sauce

He's the sauce for meat that tastes like feet!

Likes: Rotten meat
Dislikes: Lettuce
May Contain Traces Of:
Charcoal, splinters, and rust!
Rarity: Common

Awful Sauces

Awful Oyster Sauce

He smells like a fish stick and he'll make you feel sea sick.

Likes: Sea salt
Dislikes: Seaweed
May Contain Traces Of: Rust, barnacles, and oil!
Rarity: Common

Terrible Tomato Sauce

He's so rotten and sticky, it makes anything icky!

Likes: Burgers
Dislikes: Green flies
May Contain Traces Of: Tomato, grubs, and leaves!
Rarity: Common

Snot N Pepper

They're the greasy, sneezy taste sensation!

Likes: Shakin' it!
Dislikes: Bland food
May Contain Traces Of: Boogers, pepper, and tissues!
Rarity: Common

Sickly Salsa Sauce

He's the sickly salsa guaranteed to cause ulcers!

Likes: Nachos
Dislikes: Hot chilies
May Contain Traces Of: Beans, mucus, and burp!
Rarity: Rare

MOLDY VEG

watersmellin

Smell him and you'll never be the same again.

Likes: Breakfast
Dislikes: Freezers
May contain traces of: Seeds, fruit flies, and burnt skin!
Rarity: Common

Hairy Pear

He's the fruit in your lunchbox that smells like your socks!

Likes: Smelly dreadlocks
Dislikes: Hairbrushes
May contain traces of: Hair, mites, and sap!
Rarity: Ultra rare

Awful Apple

He's the perfect gift for
that teacher you hate!

Likes: Worms
Dislikes: Apple bobbing
May Contain Traces Of:
Grubs, worms, and branches!
Rarity: Ultra rare

Sour Pineapple

She's super sour and covered
in spikes. Ask yourself...
"What's to like?"

Likes: Surfing
Dislikes: Winter
May Contain Traces Of:
Beach, Hawaii, and ocean!
Rarity: Ultra rare

MOLDY VEG

CAULI-FOULER

He's the veggie that feels like a wedgie.

LIKES: Cheese
DISLIKES: Snails
MAY CONTAIN TRACES OF: Bugs, manure, and tractor!
RARITY: Ultra rare

Onion Scum

For stinging eyes and stinky breath, Onion Scum is number one!

LIKES: Making you cry
DISLIKES: Being pickled
MAY CONTAIN TRACES OF: Dirt, mud, and boots!
RARITY: Ultra rare

MUSHY MUSHROOM

He's the fungus with extra fungus!

Likes: Fungus
Dislikes: Anything that isn't fungus
May Contain Traces Of:
Fungus, fungus, and fungus!
Rarity: Ultra rare

Pukey PASSIONFRUIT

He's purple and kooky, and he'll make you want to pukey!

Likes: Puke
Dislikes: Cold weather
May Contain Traces Of:
Medicine, seeds, and fruit flies!
Rarity: Ultra rare

MOLDY VEG

SQUISHY TOMATO

He's rotten, red, and smells like he's dead!

Likes: Ketchup
Dislikes: Smelly socks
May Contain Traces Of: Seeds, ketchup, and dust!
Rarity: Ultra rare

REVOLTING SULTANA

This raisin's the dried-up grape you're sure to hate!

Likes: Sunbathing
Dislikes: Feet
May Contain Traces Of: Rotten grapes, stems, and smelly feet!
Rarity: Ultra rare

PUKING PUMPKIN

He's old, moldy, and always unclean, just right for Smelloween!

LikeS: Candy

DiSLikeS: Kids in scary costumes

MaY CONTaiN TraCeS OF:
Soil, dirt, and Halloween candy!

RariTY: Ultra rare

SOUr STrawBerry

This strawberry is as sour as they come!

LikeS: Bruises

DiSLikeS: Smoothies

MaY CONTaiN TraCeS OF:
Pesticide, ants, and soil!

RariTY: Common

STiCKY SWEETS

CHEWED CANDY

You'll get a fright with your very first bite!

Likes: Sugar
Dislikes: Tooth decay
May Contain Traces of: Dribble, teeth, and wrapper!
Rarity: Special edition

SLOBSTOPPER

He'll shut you up with his maggots and slime!

Likes: Teeth
Dislikes: Water
May Contain Traces of: Fungus, sweat, and gunk!
Rarity: Rare

MUCKY BUTTERCUP

He's a cup load of muck that's sure to suck!

Likes: Peanuts
Dislikes: Jelly
May Contain Traces of: Butter, muck, and pus!
Rarity: Special edition

SKUMMY BEAR

He's the yucky bear that comes with real hair!

Likes: Chewing gum
Dislikes: Bathing
May Contain Traces of: Lint, gum, and rubber!
Rarity: Special edition

Sticky Sweets

SLOPPY TOFFEE APPLE

He's the sloppy toffee treat that will quickly rot your teeth.

Likes: Carmel
Dislikes: Hair
May Contain Traces of: Toffee, worms, and glue!
Rarity: Common

LOLLi-SLOP

He's pre-licked for your convenience and dripping with mucus!

Likes: Tongues
Dislikes: Teeth
May Contain Traces of: Drool, nose hair, and scabs!
Rarity: Special edition

STINKY MINT

He's the mint with a smell that'll make you unwell!

Likes: Halitosis

Dislikes: Fresh breath

May Contain Traces of: Garlic, onion, and furry tongues!

Rarity: Special edition

Gooey Chewie

He's pre-chewed to slide down easy!

Likes: Being chewed

Dislikes: Being stepped on

May Contain Traces of: Phlegm, drool, and fillings!

Rarity: Special edition

Sticky Sweets

Lame Licorice

He's the licorice to choose when you're looking for ooze!

Likes: Doing the twist
Dislikes: Math
May contain traces of: Dust, oil, and toenails!
Rarity: Special edition

Smelly Bean

Where has this Smelly Bean? You don't want to know!

Likes: Traveling
Dislikes: Deodorant
May contain traces of: Fur, smells, and rotten teeth!
Rarity: Special edition

SCARY FLOSS

He's the sticky fluff that will make you feel rough.

LiKeS: Carnivals
DiSLiKeS: Rollercoasters
May Contain Traces of: Food coloring, fur, and insect legs!
Rarity: Rare

CruSTY CHOCOLATe Bar

He's got a crusty taste that lasts after it comes up fast!

LiKeS: Extreme sports
DiSLiKeS: Melting
May Contain Traces of: Mud, crusts, and Band-Aids!
Rarity: Special edition

Stinky Snacks

Gooey Nachos

His cheese probably has fleas!

Likes: Movie theaters
Dislikes: Math
May Contain Traces Of: Gunk, oil, and toenails!
Rarity: Common

Nasty Nacho

He's the corny chip snack that comes in the crushed pack!

Likes: Hot chilies
Dislikes: Sour cream
May Contain Traces Of: Nastiness, cheese, and snotamole!
Rarity: Rare

CRACKED CRACKER

Try "old" Cracked Cracker! Now in Tasty Sneeze flavor!

Likes: Moldy cheese
Dislikes: Being bored
May Contain Traces of: Mold, grease, and madness!
Rarity: Common

OOZY MUESLI BAR

He's the oozy bar that's made of lumps and festering bumps!

Likes: Going nuts
Dislikes: Milk
May Contain Traces of: Nuttiness, craziness, and ooze!
Rarity: Common

STiNKy SNacKS

corny corn DOG

Corn dog the corn slob!

Likes: Movies
Dislikes: Baths
May Contain Traces of:
Corn, grease, and
sausage dogs!
Rarity: Ultra rare

cruddy CHiP

Now with crumbs of
extra scum!

Likes: Dips
Dislikes: Diets
May Contain Traces of:
Oil, fat, and boogers!
Rarity: Common

Barf Biscuit

He goes down with a fight
and comes up all night!

Likes: Barfing
Dislikes: Getting dunked
May Contain Traces of:
Barf, dust, and crumbs!
Rarity: Common

Slop Corn

He's the snack that comes
with his own sick bucket!

Likes: Going to the movies
Dislikes: Unpopped kernels
May Contain Traces of:
Nastiness, cheese, and
snotamole!
Rarity: Common

Trashed cans

Watch out for these Limited-Edition Grosseries with a special metallic finish!

CRUDDY CAT FOOD

He's the can full of fat that's crazy about cats!

Likes: Cats
Dislikes: Cat litter
May contain traces of: Fish, grease, and furballs!
Rarity: Limited edition

CRUDDY CAT FOOD

Bad Beef can

He's the tin that belongs in the bin!

Likes: Raw meat
Dislikes: Vegans
May contain traces of: Rotting meat, milk, and pus!
Rarity: Limited edition

Slimy sardines

He's the can of fish that isn't delish!

Likes: Going fishing
Dislikes: Cats
May contain traces of: Fish bones, gills, and ocean!
Rarity: Limited edition

Limited Edition
Cruddy LOST 'N' FOUND

Unwashed Jocks

Unclean and smellin' mean!

Likes: Dark wardrobes
Dislikes: Laundry day
May Contain Traces Of:
Plastic, cotton, and moths!
Rarity: Limited edition

Rusty Car Keys

He's got rust, slime, and more,
but won't open your door!

Likes: Cars
Dislikes: Walking
May Contain Traces Of:
Metal, rust, and petrol!
Rarity: Limited edition

Scum Glasses

He's the broken pair that
doesn't care.

Likes: Eyes
Dislikes: Contact lenses
May Contain Traces Of:
Broken glass, wire, and plaster!
Rarity: Limited edition

WORTHLESS WALLET

He's bursting at the seams with bugs to make you scream!

Likes: Money
Dislikes: Pockets
May Contain Traces of: Dust, beetles, and mold!
Rarity: Limited edition

FILTHY FALSE TEETH

He's the slimy set of teeth that causes grief!

Likes: Sugar
Dislikes: Toothpaste
May Contain Traces of: Spit, old food, and decay!
Rarity: Limited edition

Dirty Money

He's the flithy wad of cash that belongs in the trash!

Likes: Gold
Dislikes: Washing machines
May Contain Traces of: Germs, gunk, and ink!
Rarity: Limited edition

GLOWING GADGETS

FLAT BATTERY

Jumpy, jittery, and constantly on edge, Flat Battery's the one who'll light up (or set fire to) any situation.

Likes: Solar power
Dislikes: Sponge baths
May contain traces of: Electrodes, chemicals, and poison!
Rarity: Special edition

Smell Phone

He's the vile cell phone that will leave you at a loss for words!

Likes: Rice
Dislikes: The toilet
May contain traces of: Glass, spit, and grime!
Rarity: Special edition

SHOCKING LIGHT BULB

He's the bright light that will give you a fright!

Likes: Electricity
Dislikes: Water
May Contain Traces Of: Glass, filament, and stunned moths!
Rarity: Special edition

FILTHY Fan

He's the filth covered fan that's leaking drool but won't leave you cool!

Likes: Humidity
Dislikes: Snow
May Contain Traces Of: Dust, metal, and flies!
Rarity: Special edition

ROTTEN RECEIPTS

Use these receipts to check off each Grossery in your collection.

RARITY KEY:

COMMON

RARE

SPECIAL EDITION

ULTRA RARE

LIMITED EDITION

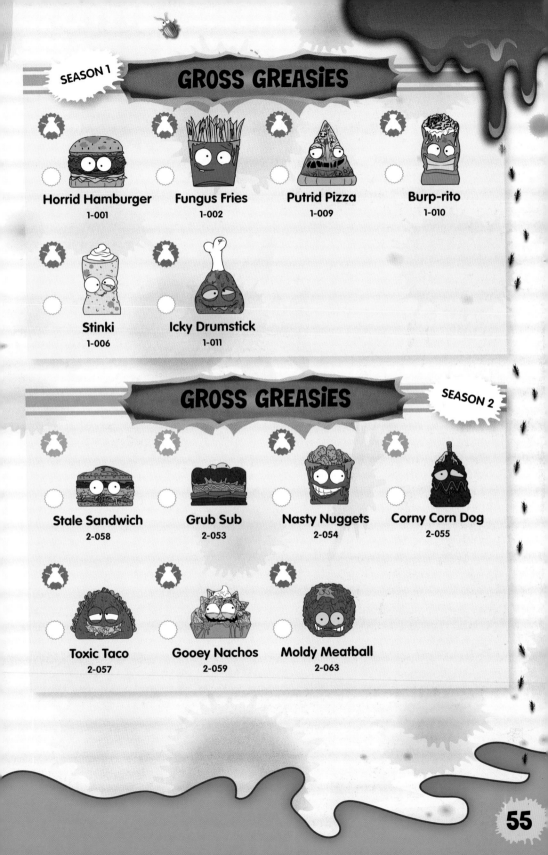

GROSS GREASIES

Horrid Hamburger
1-001

Fungus Fries
1-002

Putrid Pizza
1-009

Burp-rito
1-010

Stinki
1-006

Icky Drumstick
1-011

GROSS GREASIES

SEASON 2

Stale Sandwich
2-058

Grub Sub
2-053

Nasty Nuggets
2-054

Corny Corn Dog
2-055

Toxic Taco
2-057

Gooey Nachos
2-059

Moldy Meatball
2-063

Sour Dairy

Yuck Yogurt
1-013

Stinky Cheese
1-014

Rotten Egg
1-016

Sour Milk
1-019

Sour Dairy

Cruddy Cream
2-021

Gutter Butter
2-023

Snot Whipped Cream
2-024

Maggot Milk
2-026

Blue Spew Cheese
2-027

Mucus Milk
2-029

Pongy Parmesan
2-032

Badly Frozen

Frozen Foul
1-041

Yuck TV Dinner
1-042

Ice Scream
1-043

Unfrozen Pizza
1-044

Half-Baked Bakery

Tasteless Tart
1-022

Rotten Apple Pie
1-025

Le Crusty Croissant
1-027

Barf Bagel
1-026

Awful Waffle
1-029

Dodgey Donut
1-030

Stale Muffin
1-032

Chunky Cheesecake
1-033

Putrid Pancakes
1-037

Stinky Snacks

Slop Corn
1-081

Oozy Muesli Bar
1-084

Pukey Cookie
1-087

Knot Nice Pretzel
1-088

Cracked Cracker
1-090

Cruddy Chip
1-091

Barf Biscuit
1-093

Nasty Nacho
1-094

AwfuL Sauces

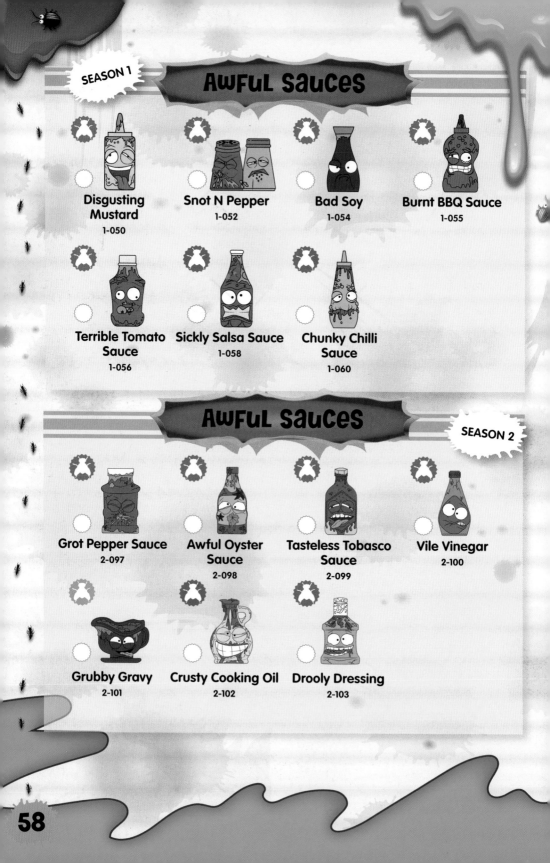

Disgusting Mustard
1-050

Snot N Pepper
1-052

Bad Soy
1-054

Burnt BBQ Sauce
1-055

Terrible Tomato Sauce
1-056

Sickly Salsa Sauce
1-058

Chunky Chilli Sauce
1-060

AwfuL Sauces

SEASON 2

Grot Pepper Sauce
2-097

Awful Oyster Sauce
2-098

Tasteless Tobasco Sauce
2-099

Vile Vinegar
2-100

Grubby Gravy
2-101

Crusty Cooking Oil
2-102

Drooly Dressing
2-103

SCUMMY SODAS

SEASON 1

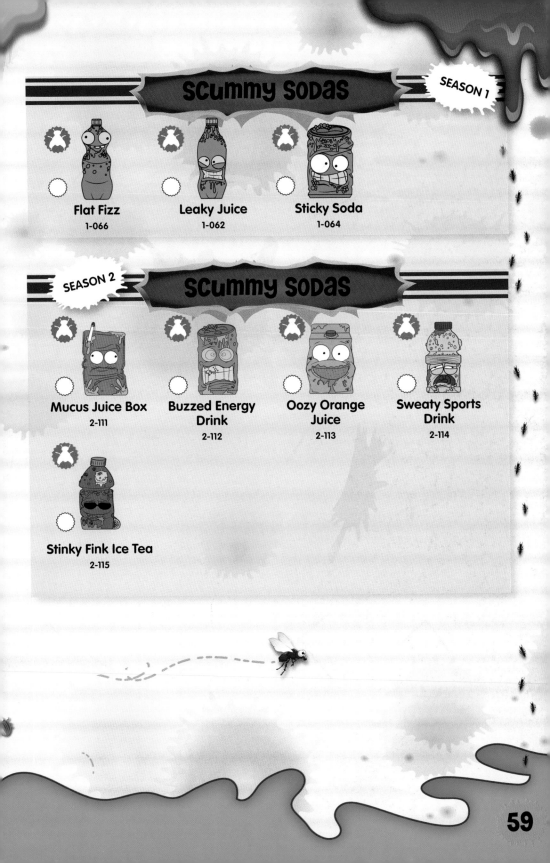

Flat Fizz
1-066

Leaky Juice
1-062

Sticky Soda
1-064

SEASON 2

SCUMMY SODAS

Mucus Juice Box
2-111

Buzzed Energy Drink
2-112

Oozy Orange Juice
2-113

Sweaty Sports Drink
2-114

Stinky Fink Ice Tea
2-115

Barf-Room Supplies

Grotty Soap
1-067

Shampoop
1-068

Rough Toilet Paper
1-069

Rotting Toothpaste
1-070

Spotty Zit Cream
1-071

Leaky Sunscreen
1-079

Snot Good Tissues
1-080

Barf-Room Supplies

SEASON 2

Sewer Glove
2-035

Splodgy Spray Can
2-038

Scummy Sponge
2-039

Mucus Mouth Wash
2-040

Icky Eyedrops
2-041

Stinky Aftershave
2-042

Shonky Shoving Brush
2-044

Bald Hair Brush
2-045

MOLDY VeG

Hairy Pear
1-097

Cauli-fouler
1-101

Squishy Tomato
1-105

Shoccoli
1-110

Sour Pineapple
1-111

Awful Apple
1-112

Onion Scum
1-114

Red Hot Chilli
1-115

Mushy Mushroom
1-116

Smashed Potato
1-118

Revolting Sultana
1-119

Puking Pumpkin
1-120

TRASHeD cans

Bad Beef Can
1-145

Sloppy Soup Tin
1-148

Slimy Sardines
1-146

Tinned Slimeapple
1-149

Cruddy Cat Food
1-147

Faked Beanz
1-150

STICKY SWEETS

Stinky Mint
1-124

Gooey Chewie
1-127

Lolli-slop
1-128

Lame Licorice
1-130

Heartless Candy
1-131

Crusty Chocolate Bar
1-132

Chewed Candy
1-133

Mucky Buttercup
1-134

Gooey Smooch
1-135

Faulty Malty
1-137

Skummy Bear
1-138

Smelly Bean
1-141

UNTASTY TREATS

Ginger Dread Man
2-066

Sloppy Toffee Apple
2-067

Car-Rot Cake
2-069

Yuck Éclair
2-073

Scary Floss
2-076

Slobstopper
2-078

Barf Brownie
2-079

Mushmellow Crispy
2-080

GLOWIN' GADGETS

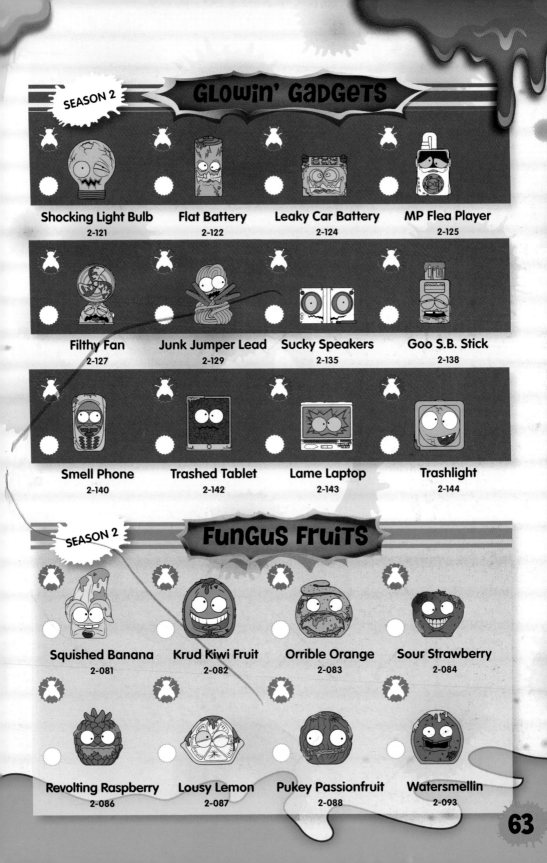

Shocking Light Bulb
2-121

Flat Battery
2-122

Leaky Car Battery
2-124

MP Flea Player
2-125

Filthy Fan
2-127

Junk Jumper Lead
2-129

Sucky Speakers
2-135

Goo S.B. Stick
2-138

Smell Phone
2-140

Trashed Tablet
2-142

Lame Laptop
2-143

Trashlight
2-144

FunGuS FruiTS

Squished Banana
2-081

Krud Kiwi Fruit
2-082

Orrible Orange
2-083

Sour Strawberry
2-084

Revolting Raspberry
2-086

Lousy Lemon
2-087

Pukey Passionfruit
2-088

Watersmellin
2-093

SEASON 2

GOOEY BREAKFASTS

Rancid Raisin Toast
2-001

Soggy Teabag
2-004

Muck Muffin
2-005

Slop Tart
2-007

Weevil Cereal
2-008

Peanut Splutter
2-009

Scummy Honey
2-010

Busted Eggs
2-013

Pukey Pancake Mix
2-012

Horrible Hash Brown
2-016

SEASON 2

Limited Edition
Cruddy LOST 'N' Found

Rusty Car Keys
2-145

Unwashed Jocks
2-146

Scum Glasses
2-147

Worthless Wallet
2-148

Filthy False Teeth
2-149

Dirty Money
2-150